I'm going to give you a Polar Bear Hug!

By Caroline B. Cooney

Illustrated by Tim Warnes

ZONDERkidz

For Ari and Tali x
—TM

ZONDERKIDZ

I'm Going to Give You a Polar Bear Hug
Copyright © 2020 by Caroline B. Cooney
Illustrations © 2020 by Tim Warnes

Requests for information should be addressed to:
Zonderkidz, 3900 *Sparks Dr. SE, Grand Rapids, Michigan 49546*

ISBN 978-0-310-76870-8 (hardcover)
ISBN 978-0-310-76873-9 (ebook)

Library of Congress Cataloging-in-Publication Data

Zondervan titles may be purchased in bulk for educational, business, fundraising, or sales promotional use. For information, please email SpecialMarkets@Zondervan.com.

Art direction: Cindy Davis/Ron Huizinga

Printed in China

20 21 22 23 24 DSC 10 9 8 7 6 5 4 3 2 1

I'm going to give you a polar bear hug.

A wintry, windy,
play in the snow hug.

A shivery, quivery,
forty below hug.

I'm going to give you a fox hug.

A chase your tail,

Laugh at the gale,

Dance down the trail hug.

I'm going to give you a seal hug.

A whiskers and nose,

Laugh when it snows,

My toes are froze hug.

I'm going to give you a snow bunny hug.
A tickly, funny,
Soft and sunny,

Sweet as honey hug.

I'm going to give you a reindeer hug.
A race through the snow
From antlers to toe,

Ready, set, go! hug.

I'm going to give you a cardinal hug.
A high in the sky,
Wave good-bye,

Come on, let's fly! hug.

I'm going to give you a penguin hug.

A fishy grin,
Black and white spin,
Dance flipper-to-chin hug.

I'm going to give you a walrus hug.
An out on the ice floe,
Wow! Does the wind blow!

Where did your hat go, hug.

I'm going to give you a goose hug.
A hold tight to that feather,
It's such icy weather,

Let's stick together hug.

And you will give me,
As you sit on my knee,
Hugs from the North Pole
surrounded by ice,

Hugs we do once and hugs we do twice.

Hugs in cradles, cribs, and chairs,
Hugs with one and hugs in pairs,
Hugs that take away all our cares,

Hugs with all those polar bears!